To my son Nicolaus, who always asked me to read just a little bit more each night.

The Adventures of Miki the Narwhal

As it happens, there is a little narwhal named Miki who lives with his mother and father, his sister Nora and the rest of his family near the North Pole, in the Arctic Ocean around the islands of Franz Josef Land.

During the winter the family swims offshore in the ocean, near the pack ice in very deep water.

Here, there is plenty of food for everyone.

The older narwhals are able to dive over half of a mile deep to find a meal, because they can hold their breath.

Miki and Nora are still too little to dive that deep and have to find their food closer to the surface.

One day towards the end of the winter, the family was swimming closer to the islands.

Miki caught a glimpse of land out of the corner of his eye.

"What's that?" he asked.

"That is a place that you must never go until the spring comes," was the loud reply from his father.

The next day Miki talked about what it was that he saw with his sister Nora.

Nora had also seen the island and was told by her mother that it was a place to go in the spring, and that in no way was she to swim there without the rest of the family.

They were both very curious about this thing called land.

After the sun went down Miki could not sleep, his imagination was filled with thoughts about what the "island" was and what special things might be there.

It looked like it wasn't that far away; maybe a one-hour swim and he could be there.

He made up his mind to try it.

He waited for daybreak, and when the water started to brighten, he started to swim!

After the day had begun the entire family started to have their first meal.

A school of squid had ventured past, one of the narwhal's favorite treats.

The feasting lasted about two hours.

In the frenzy the family didn't notice that Miki was not there eating with them.

By the time they did, he had already been gone for at least two hours!

Where was Miki? They had to find him!

They devised a plan to swim in circles that were wider and wider and explore all the channels, even though it was very dangerous, until he was found.

Miki had never been away from the family before, but he was so excited that he didn't even think about them.

He swam and swam until he saw the coastline ahead.

He was beginning to get tired and was already hungry, but kept on swimming towards the beach.

The water was getting more and more covered with ice, but he did not notice.

He found a channel he thought would lead him closer to the island and started up it.

After about five minutes he was ready to take a breath of air. He tried to get to the surface but there was a thick layer of ice on the water.

He could not break through the ice to breathe.

Miki was trapped!

Miki tried not to panic…

Then he remembered that his father had showed him how to hold his breath a little longer each time he went to the surface.

He thought if he could swim a little more and hold his breath a little longer… there might be a hole in the ice that would be open to the sky.

He couldn't see anything!

Just as he was about to give up and try to go back he saw a small opening ahead.

He jumped to full speed and at last got to the surface.

He took a deep breath and almost collapsed as he went back for another.

He never felt so good and the air never was as sweet.

After he rested a bit he went to the surface again…

Suddenly he saw a creature that he had never seen before.

"Where am I?" asked Miki.

The walrus answered, "You are where a little narwhal should not be."

"Didn't your family tell you not to come so far inland this time of the year?"

Miki had to tell him the truth.

He had not listened to his father and tried to explore the island alone.

The walrus explained to Miki that no narwhals came inland during the winter because all of the channels and estuaries were frozen with a thick layer of ice that does not allow for a place to come up for air.

"The opening that you are in is mine and I have to swim in it all the time to keep it from freezing."

"Not many narwhals make it back to open water and their family, you are a very lucky little narwhal indeed," said the walrus.

Miki was scared.

"Please, tell me what should I do?"

"You must try your hardest to swim back to open water, before the sun goes down and the ice becomes thicker."

That meant that Miki must hold his breath longer than he had ever done, and swim stronger than ever before to make it home.

"I can do it!" he said to himself.

Miki took the deepest breath he ever had taken, ducked below the ice and started to swim towards home.

He was swimming and swimming for what seemed like forever and still did not see the sunlight through the water, the ice thick over his head.

Miki was swimming faster and deeper than he ever had.

The only thing he was thinking about was getting back to his family and how he would feel when he finally got there.

After at least twenty minutes, which is a very long time, he saw the bright water in the far distance.

Within a minute he was able to rush to the surface.

Gasping for air, he took the deepest breath ever, then rolled over and floated on his back in exhaustion.

He couldn't have been there for more than a minute before his Father, Mother and Nora swam up to him.

They all hugged and kissed him (in their narwhal way).

Before any of them could ask anything, Miki shouted, "I'm sorry, I should have listened to you, you had a good reason to tell me not to go to the island during the winter."

Miki was the happiest ever to be back with his family.

Nora was filled with questions and could not wait for him to tell them about his adventure.

But all of that would have to wait, little narwhals all need to nap… especially a very tired and happy Miki.

Printed in Great Britain
by Amazon.co.uk, Ltd.,
Marston Gate.